D1635715

*The books in
the Sparklers series
are designed to give
pleasure to young readers
when, having achieved a high
level of confidence, they have an
unrelenting demand
for new and more challenging stories.*

Tilman Röhrig

Tina in Hiding

Translated by
Alisa Jaffa
Illustrated by
Manfred Limmroth

Burke

CIP data
Röhrig, Tilman
  Tina in Hiding
  I. Title II. Tina im Schrank. *English.* –(Sparklers)
  III. Series
  833'.914 [J] PZ7

  ISBN 0 222 01106 8 Hardbound
  ISBN 0 222 01078 9 Paperback

Burke Publishing Company Limited
Pegasus House, 116-120 Golden Lane, London EC1Y OTL, England.
Burke Publishing (Canada) Limited   *Registered Office:*
20 Queen Street West, Suite 3000, Box 30, Toronto, Canada M5H 1V5.
Burke Publishing Company Inc.   *Registered Office:*
333 State Street, PO Box 1740, Bridgeport, Connecticut 06601, U.S.A.
Filmset by Graphiti (Hull) Ltd., Hull, England.
Printed in Germany by Richterdruck, Würzburg.

It's Monday and Tom says,
"I can wash up fast.
Much faster than
you can dry."
He stands at the sink
in the kitchen, grinning.
The mountain of foam
on the steaming washing-up water
pops and bubbles and climbs right over
the edge of the green bowl.
Tina waits impatiently
beside her big brother.
Tina laughs.

6

"You'll see! Just you wait!"
And she whirls the red and white teacloth
round and round her head like a propellor.
Tom sinks the dirty knives,
the dirty forks and the dirty spoons
into the foam mountain.
Now he takes the plates
and lets them slide into the bowl.
They gurgle in the water
like huge sea creatures.
"Ready!" calls Tom
and waves the washing-up brush in the air.
"Steady!" shouts Tina,
and shoots out her hand to the plate-rack.
"Go!" they both yell together.
With a splash Tom smacks the brush
into the water.
The bubbles fly
over the edge of the bowl.

"Faster.

Hurry up with that plate!"

Tina eggs her brother on.

The water slurps.

The bristles scrub.

"First one done."

Tom puts the clean plate

in the plate rack.

The soapy water drips down.

Quickly, Tina snatches

at the warm, wet plate.

The water slops.

The bristles scrub.

The teacloth rubs.

Done!

As Tom lifts the second plate

out of the water,

Tina sets her dry, white plate

on the kitchen table.

Tom grins.
Tina beams.
The score is one all.
Washing-up is fun today.

In the room next door
Mother is still feeding
baby Fergus.
The door is ajar.
Fergus is one and a half.
When there's no spinach for tea
their little brother
can manage very well
on his own.
But when it's spinach
Mother has to feed him.
Tom is Tina's older brother.
Tom is twelve
and Tina is nine.

Earlier on Mother had said
"You big ones can do
the washing-up today."
The water slurps.
The bristles scrub.
Now the next plate
is in the plate rack.
The soapy water drips.
Tina polishes away. Faster!
Still she hasn't finished.
Faster, faster.
"I'm winning," shouts Tom.
"Two-one to me."
Tina plonks her plate
down on the table.
"I must catch up with Tom,"
she thinks.
Hastily she grabs
at the next wet plate.

10

It is slippery.
"Tina, be careful!
Don't break anything!"
warns Mother
from next door.
"I *am* being careful,"
says Tina,
But her hold on the plate
isn't tight enough.
Slowly the plate slips
out of her grasp.
She makes a wild grab
at it but she only
 brushes the rim
with the teacloth.
The white plate
spins through
the air.

It nearly lands on the table.
Nearly!
But then it slides off the edge
and crashes to the floor.

12

The shattered pieces flew apart.
The shock
made Tina freeze.
Her mouth gaped open.
Tom's eyes were riveted
to the kitchen floor.

Mother's voice called
from the next room
"Tina! Can't you be careful?"
Tina came back to life.
She pressed the teacloth
to her mouth.
Mother came in with Fergus on her arm.
He had a green spinach circle
round his mouth.
Mother's blouse was spattered
with green spinach spots.

Tina thought to herself,

"Don't they look funny!"

But the plate lay smashed to
smithereens on the kitchen floor.

"Better not laugh now,"

thought Tina.

She stammered, "I... I..."

She couldn't think of anything else.

Tom stammered, "I... I..."

He couldn't think of anything else.

Fergus opened his mouth and crowed:

"Pate boken. Pate boken."

Mother scolded,

"That nice plate!"

Tina looked at Mother helplessly.

Tom got the better of his stammers and
bravely he said,

"We both did it."

Gratefully, Tina thought:

14

"Sometimes Tom is
a really kind, big brother."
But Mother shook her head.
"No, Tom. That isn't true!
It was Tina who
dropped the plate on the floor."
Tina took a deep breath.
She felt like answering back,
but Mother sighed,
"Tina, you are clumsy!"
The words stung.
Suddenly, Tina had nothing left to say.
Without a word,
she breathed out again in a rush.
But the thoughts raced through her mind.
"We were only having a game.
I didn't mean to drop the plate.
It slipped out of my hand.
I'm *not* clumsy."

Tina took another deep breath
and opened her mouth.
But Mother looked at her
and shook her head worriedly.
Because Mother did nothing
except shake her head,
Tina was even more upset.
Without a word, she breathed out.
But inside her head
there was a loud banging.
Clumsy. Bang.
Clumsy. Bang.
Bang. Clumsy.
Bang.
Louder and louder.
In a rage, Tina slapped the teacloth
down on the kitchen table.
Tom broke in quickly, saying:
"I'll sweep up the pieces."

But Tina rushed out of the kitchen.
She slammed the door,
and stormed across the hall.
She went into the bedroom
and slammed the door behind her
with a loud crash.
She threw herself onto her bed.
Then she grabbed her
stuffed grey elephant
by the trunk
and hurled him
at the big wardrobe.
"Floppy Ears! You are clumsy!"
she cried.

With both hands
Tina gathered up her quilt
and sent it
flying across the room,
to land in front of Fergus' cot

"Clumsy!"
Tina is quite a strong girl.
She clenched her fists
and pummelled her pillow.

She carried on until she had pummelled
all her rage and strength
into the pillow.
Then she sank back
on to her bed, exhausted.

On the wall
hangs a large picture of a horse.

18

Its brown eyes
gazed down sadly at Tina.

"I'm not clumsy,"
whispered Tina to the horse.
"You understand me, don't you?"

The big, beautiful, brown eyes
stared back at her.
Floppy Ears lay on the floor.
Tina bent down
and stroked his big ears
and his long trunk.
"You're not clumsy, either.
There are no clumsy people here."

Tina picked Floppy Ears up
and carried him
over to the big wardrobe.

Behind the right-hand door
were Tina's clothes.

She climbed up on a chair.
The big key to the wardrobe door
lay on top of the wardrobe.
Mother had hidden it there
so that Fergus did not play with it.
Tina took the key
and opened the left-hand door
of the big wardrobe.
It creaked.
The winter clothes hang here
and on the shelves
there are thick winter socks.

"I'm taking you with me,"
Tina whispered into the elephant's
right ear.

She stepped into the wardrobe
and stood among the winter clothes.
She took hold of the lock
from the inside
and pulled the door shut.
It creaked again.
Inside the wardrobe
it was quite dark.
The winter clothes had
such a comforting smell.
Tina crouched down
and crept about among the things
right into the far corner.
This is her secret hiding-place.
"Don't be frightened, Floppy Ears,
I'll put the light on."
She groped about
for the torch and—click.
A bright beam lit up the darkness.

"That surprised you, didn't it?"
whispered Tina
as she shone the torch
over her secret stores.
There was a bag of caramels—
and a half-full bottle of lemonade.
But the box of chocolate buttons was
empty.

Right in the far corner
sat Tina's favourite doll.
She used to be able to open her eyes.
But she can't any more.
"Look, Floppy Ears,
this is my secret hiding-place,"
Tina whispered
to the stuffed, grey elephant.
She switched off the torch
and rocked Floppy Ears in her arms.

It's Tuesday and Mother says,
"Tina, it's your turn to take Fergus
to the playground this afternoon."
Tina looks at her Mother.
"I can't" she says.
"I'm busy."
Mother sighs.

Tina plucked up all her courage
and said,
"Tom promised me
I could play football with the others."
Mother pleaded with a smile.
"But Tina,
You are Fergus' big sister.
Let Tom play football today,
and you two little ones
can go to the playground."
Tina nodded,

24

but she stopped listening.
She thought to herself:
"When it comes to washing-up,
I belong to the big ones.
When Fergus has to go to the playground,
then I'm one of the little ones.
It's all right for Tom.
He is always the big one.
It's all right for Fergus, too.
He is always the little one.
It's only me that has to keep swopping
about.
One day Mother says,
'The two big ones can tidy up.'
Another time Father says,
'The two little ones
should have been in bed long ago.'
And only Tom is allowed
to watch the football on television."

Mother slipped a vest
over Fergus' head
and put a clean nappy on him.
The fasteners crackled
and Fergus' bottom
was soon like a soft bundle.
Over the top
Mother put the blue dungarees.
Fergus was ready.
"Let him play in the sandpit,"
Mother said.

Tina took big steps
as she pushed the pram.
The small wheels rattled and bumped
over the pavement.
The spare nappy
was tucked behind the seat.
Fergus kicked his feet with glee.

The sun
painted the dark shadow
of the pram
onto the paving stones.
At each step
Tina tried to tread
on the black patch.
But the pram had moved on
and taken its shadow
with it.

The playground
is on the edge of the
estate. Tina looked round.
Nothing but
stupid climbing-frames,
benches and the sand-pit.
Stupid mothers and stupid children.

Fergus waved his arms about.
Slowly, Tina
pushed the pram
past the playground.
Fergus shouted:
"Pay! Dare! Pay!"
"Shut up!" scolded Tina.
She pushed the pram
past the bushes
over to the big field.
Tom was playing football
with Terry, Daniel
and Charlie.
A gate was their goal.
And Tanya was goalie!
She had real shin-pads on.
She dived at the ball
like a real goalie
on television.

"Tom! There's your sister!"

called Daniel.

Everyone cheered.

"Now we can play properly.

Three against three."

Tina asked,

"What shall I do with Fergus?"

Tom said,

"He can play in the grass.

We'll be able to keep an eye on him!"

Tom was pleased

that Tina had come after all.

"Well" thought Tina,

"Fergus would only get dirty

in the sand-pit.

The grass is much cleaner."

"I'm coming!"

she called to her friends.

Then she lifted Fergus out of the pram

and put him down on the grass.
Tina bent down
and pointed to a daisy.
"Now, Fergus, you pick
lots and lots of flowers."
Immediately Fergus started
crawling through the grass.
With his chubby, little fingers
he picked a daisy.
He held it out to Tina.
"Fower," chuckled Fergus.
Tina pointed to the
hundreds of white daisies.
"You must pick them all. All of them."
Fergus crawled on through the grass
and reached out for the daisies
with both hands.

Tina, Daniel and Tom were playing
against Tanya, Charlie and Terry.
Every one of them was a refereee.
Easy, since the score was nil - nil.
Daniel had the ball.
He passed to Tom. *Shoot.*
And Tanya dived into the corner.
She threw herself
on top of the ball.
Goal-kick.
Charlie dribbled.
He lost the ball to Daniel.
Then Terry got the ball,
dodged round Charlie,
and forward,
past Tom. *Shoot.*
Tina ran towards the ball,
and ducked down.
The ball was fast and....

Goal!

Tanya, Charlie and Terry cheered.

One—nil to the others.

Tom ran over to Tina in a fury.

"You have to throw yourself on the ball,
just like Tanya.

Or we'll lose."

Tina shouted back,

"But Tanya's got shin-pads.

And I haven't. It's not fair!"

"Oh, you're stupid!" said Tom.

He turned his back on her,
and ran back
into the middle of the field.

They started again.

The four boys fought for the ball.

Dribble. *Shoot.*

Trip. Run.

"Go on, pass!"

Tina was angry.
"How can I dive for the ball
if I haven't got shin-pads?"

Tom and Daniel
thundered up to Tanya's gate.
Charlie and Terry
defended it grimly.

Tina looked across the field.
Fergus was
crouching in the grass
picking daisies.
His nappy-wrapped bottom
looked like a football.

At the far end of the field
Daniel was about to score.
But now Tanya had the ball.

"Wait," yelled Tina.
"I'll be back in a second!"

Tina ran over to Fergus.
His right hand was
full of daisy-heads.
"Fower," gurgled Fergus,
and stretched out his hands.
"Come on, Fergus, stand up!"
Tina pulled her
little brother
to his feet.

In two seconds
she took of his dungarees.
Rip! Rip!
The nappy fastening was undone.
Thank goodness!
It was still dry.

Tina took off the nappy.
She folded the narrow part under,
and lay the nappy
across her right knee.
The fastenings crackled into place.
One shin-pad.
"It fits!" laughed Tina triumphantly,
and sat Fergus in the grass.
"Go on—pick lots more flowers!"

Her little brother
was much happier
without his nappy.
He waddled off to the next daisy.
His bare bottom shone brightly
in the sunshine.

Tina ran over to the pram
and took the spare nappy
out of the pocket behind the seat.
She folded the narrow end under
and fitted the nappy round her left knee.
"Fits!" Tina cheered
and ran back to her goal.

The boys and Tanya laughed.
"Great idea!"
Tom clapped his hands.
"Let's play,"
yelled Tina.
She stalked to and fro
along her goal line like a tiger.
The game raged in
the centre of the field.
Charlie broke through the defence
and thundered up to Tina's goal. *Shoot.*

With a yell

Tina threw herself at the ball.

The shin-pads hit the grass.

"Held," laughed Tina.

Nothing hurt.

Terrific!

What a brilliant game of football.

The sun shone.

Kick off. Dribble, pass, *shoot*.

Tanya wasn't watching the ball and—

the score was one all.

The game went to and fro.

But where was Fergus!

Right at the far end of the field

she saw the gleam of his bare bottom.

"Fergus! Come here immediately!"

yelled Tina.

Her baby brother didn't hear her.

The game stopped.

Tina ran across the pitch.

and carried Fergus

back to the edge of the field.

"Stay there, like a good boy, Fergus!"

Her little brother had no flowers

left in his hand.

Instead, a circle of white flower heads

had grown around his mouth.

His lips were yellow from the pollen.

Off he went again.

His chubby, little fingers

grasped at the flowers

and pulled off the heads.

"Fower," Fergus gurgled

and stuffed a handful

into his mouth.

"Goal!" The score was two—one
with Tina's team winning.
Kick-off. Dribble.
The ball went to and fro.
Pass. *Shoot.*

The afternoon passed.
At the finish, the score was eleven all.
Everyone had won!

Where was Fergus?
The bare bottom was over there.
Tina caught the crawling bundle.
She put his dungarees back on.

The nappies were dirty
and torn to shreds.
On the way home
Tina stuffed them in a waste-bin.

Tom and the others
rode past on their bikes.
They waved to Tina.
Eleven—eleven!
What a game!
Fergus sat
quite still in the pram.
He didn't wave his arms.
He didn't kick his legs.
His mouth was one huge daisy.

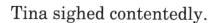

Tina sighed contentedly.
A great game.
Fergus sighed.
He made a noise.
Then he laughed softly.

At the front door
Tina lifted her little brother
out of his pram.
Then she discovered the mess.
All those daisies had been playing
football in Fergus' stomach!
They rumbled round in his little tummy
and caused a terrible commotion.
And then it was too late.
Without a nappy, it was much too late!
"Oh, Fergus!"
Tina saw and smelled the mess.
"Oh, Fergus,
you are a mess!"
Fergus chuckled with pleasure.
Tina didn't laugh.
Carefully, she carried
Fergus up the stairs
and rang the door bell.

"But what did you do with Fergus' nappies?
I really don't understand you," said Mother.
Tina looked at Mother helplessly.
"Please answer,
when I ask you a question."
"We were only playing football,"
Tina tried to explain.
"Where? In the playground?"
"I mustn't tell lies," thought Tina.
She said in a quiet voice,
"No, in the field."
"But I still don't understand.
What happened to the nappies!"
Mother picked up
the dirty dungarees
with the tips of two fingers
and dropped them in some cold water.
"I needed the nappies,"
Tina tried to explain.

"But that's absurd!" said Mother,
She had no idea
Of the different uses of nappies.
Tina nodded her head.
"Yes, I did."
Things had gone too far for Mother.
"That's quite enough.
I don't believe a word of it.
Go straight to your room.
You are a great worry to me, Tina."
Mother heaved a deep, worried sigh.

Without a word
Tina turned
and ran into the bedroom.
The horse on the wall
gazed down sadly at her
with its big, brown eyes.

44

Slowly, Tina pulled the chair
up to the big wardrobe.
she climbed up on it
and took down the key.
The left-hand door creaked.
Tina pulled it shut behind her.
In the dark corner
she cuddled her favourite doll.
"I don't want to be a worry to Mother,"
she whispered.
"But everything I do
seems to be wrong."
Tina hugged the doll.
"Nobody loves me," she whispered.
And the tears
rolled slowly down
her cheeks.

It's Wednesday, and Tina says
to her friend Tanya,
"I still have
some pocket money left."
"Well?"
The tip of Tina's tongue
darts across her lips
from one corner
of her mouth to the other.
"I've got some, too," says Tanya.
She pushes out
the tip of her tongue
and, with a sudden slurp,
it disappears
inside her mouth.
I know,"
says Tanya.
"Let's buy ice-cream
for each of us."

46

Tina dashed off
with Tanya close behind her.
When you fancy
an ice-cream,
your feet run
much faster than usual.
It's ice-starvation.
The two of them soon
reached the shopping precinct.
By the time they went through
the door of
the ice-cream parlour,
their mouths were dry as dust.
"Lemon and raspberry,
in a large cone, please,"
ordered Tanya.
"Vanilla and chocolate
in a large cone, please,"
ordered Tina.

Two scoops of ice-cream
sat side by side
on top of Tina's cone.
Very carefully
Tina licked one side.
Ice-cold and vanilla sweet.
Now a lick on
the other side,
and her lips were cold with chocolate.
Now the two scoops
were squashed together
in the cone.
Tanya and Tina
sat down on a bench,
by the flower-beds.
You need
peace and quiet
to eat ice-cream.

48

"Let's have a taste!"
Tina leaned over to Tanya
and licked
the yellow scoop of lemon.
In return,
her friend's tongue
made a groove
in Tina's chocolate.
"Yummy!"
said Tina and Tanya together.
By now the ice-cream
was getting softer.
Just right.
Now the whole tongue
could set to work.
Four licks and the two scoops
squeezed together.
A pointed ice-cream hat
perched on the cone.

Another lick and the point had gone.
It melted in the mouth
and then slid down, sweet and delicious.
Suddenly, a hungry wasp
buzzed round Tina's head.
With her free hand,
Tina flapped at the unwanted pest.
"I'm pushing my ice-cream into the cone,"
announced Tanya.
Tina nodded, "Me too."
Both of them pushed
at their ice-cream mountains
with their tongues.
Both of them stretched out
and rested their heads comfortably
against the bench.
They sucked the tip of the cone
until it was soft,
and then bit off the end.

There comes that wasp again!
"Stupid thing," scolded Tanya
and flapped at the nuisance
with her free hand.

The ice-cream melted
and dripped from the bottom
of the cone.
Now it tasted like
delicious chocolate-and-
vanilla-flavoured milk.
"Mine's empty."
Tanya sighed contentedly.
"So is mine," said Tina.

They both crunched
the cornets
and ate the last
of the ice-cream wafer.
"When it's my birthday
I'm going to ask
for ice-cream
every day
for a year," said Tina.
"When is your birthday!"
asked Tanya.
Tina sighed.
"Not till December.
And by then I always forget.
If only my birthday
was in summer,
that's what I'd ask for."
The wasp zig-zagged
round their heads.

Tanya and Tina
flapped their hands wildly.
They ran for a bit.
But the wasp buzzed
right by their ears.
"Stupid thing!" "Go away!" "Buzz off!"

All of a sudden the buzzing stopped.
"Where's it gone?"
asked Tina breathlessly,
and spun round in a circle.
"Tina," screamed Tanya
and pointed to Tina's arm.
The wasp!

Tina shook her arm.

"Ooooow!" she howled

The sting was so painful,

like a thousand pricking needles.

Tina screamed,

the sting was still stinging.

But the wasp flew off,

pleased with its work.

The mean creature!

Tanya wanted to see the arm.

But someone looking at it

made it hurt even more.

Tina ran home.

She howled—like a fire-engine

stuck on one note.

People jumped out of her way.

Tanya ran along

after her.

"Muuuuummy!"
echoed through the hall.
"Muuuuummy!"
The sound came
up the stairs.
When Tina screams in misery
Mother always
hears immediately.
She came to the door
of the flat
and ran down a few stairs
to meet Tina.
"Muuuuummy!"
Tina rushed up,
and Mother put her arms
round her.
"Mummy!"
Tanya was quite out of breath.
"Tina's been stung by a wasp!" she gasped.

The screams got louder,

and Tina stretched out her arm.

A red bump

had appeared on it.

"Come along. Tina.

Let's put some cream on the sting"

Mother led Tina up

the rest of the stairs.

Tanya stayed behind.

"I have to go home."

Mother looked at Tanya gratefully.

"It was nice of you to bring

Tina back home."

But Tanya shook her head.

"Well, we're friends, aren't we?"

"Bye, Tanya,"

gulped Tina through her tears.

"Bye, Tina!"

Tanya ran down the stairs.

"Wasp! Wasp!"

crowed Fergus,

and pulled at Tina's trousers.

Tina stamped her foot.

"Stop it, Fergus! Be quiet."

"Wasp! Wasp."

Fergus continued to shout.

"That's enough, now, Fergus,"

Mother scolded.

Instantly, the baby stopped.

Tina sobbed,

and rested her head

against Mother again.

Then Mother had an idea.

"Come with me to the kitchen, Tina!"

"What? No cream?"

Tina pointed at the big bump.
It was getting bigger
by the minute.
"I know a good cure."
Mother ruffled
Tina's hair.
She took a knife
and peeled an onion.
"Look, Tina.
Now I'm crying, too."
Mother smiled as the onion tears
ran down her cheeks.
Tina stroked
Mother's back
to comfort her.
Mother placed two onion rings
on the red bump.
Then she covered the place
with a beautiful white bandage.

The wasp sting didn't hurt
quite so much any more.
Tina stared at the thick bandage.
"Am I very ill?"
she asked, and held
her arm out stiffly,
as if it were in plaster.
"A wasp sting can be quite nasty."
Mother smiled sympathetically.

"Perhaps I ought to go
and lie down for a bit,"
sighed Tina,
and made her way slowly
across the hall.
Fergus waddled along behind her.

When she got to the bedroom,
Tina looked at the big wardrobe.
"No, I don't need
my secret hiding-place today,"
she said to the horse on the wall.
Very carefully, Tina lay down
on her bed.
She put her bandaged arm
across her stomach.
Fergus crawled up on the bed.
He was very curious
about the white bandage.
"Ow?" he asked.
Tina nodded.
"I'm very ill," she said.
Her little brother
bent over her arm,
took a deep breath and blew.
"Better?" he asked.

60

"Not a bit."
Fergus took another deep breath
and puffed hard.
"Better now?"
"A little"
Fergus blew so hard
that drops of spit spluttered
on the bandage.
"Better now?"
"Nearly." Tina smiled weakly.
She took Floppy Ears
and sat him
next to the wasp-arm.

She spread his trunk
protectively across the bandage,
right over the bump.
Fergus crawled to Tina's other side,
till his head
lay next to Tina's shoulder.
He put his thumb and finger
in his mouth,
closed his eyes and sucked.

"It's nice," thought Tina.
"Floppy Ears and Fergus are nice.
Mother is nice."
She spun out the *i*
sound in her mind: ni-i-ice.
"The wasp is a pest,
but Tanya is nice."
Fergus sniffed.
Tina fell asleep.

It's Thursday evening and Father says,
"Mother and I are going out.
The Sullivans are having
a Midsummer party.
Fergus must go to bed straight
after tea.
Tom and Tina may stay up
and watch television till nine o'clock."
"Tom, look after
your brother and sister!"
says Mother.
She is wearing her bright
butterfly dress.
Father is wearing a freshly-ironed shirt.
"The Sullivans' telephone number
is next to the telephone.
Just in case."
The door of the flat closes,
and Mother and Father are gone.

Tom nudged Tina. "Guess what?
We'll have a party, too.
A cosy television party."
Tina clapped her hands.
"With lemonade and peanuts."

All that was left of the wasp sting
was a red dot. The onion rings
were a great help.

But what's the use of
a television party,
when there's nothing on
except the boring news?
On the other channel
there were some people sitting round a table
just talking.
From time to time
each of them took a drink of water.

Tom and Tina watched carefully.

A woman took a drink.

"Cheers!"

they shouted at the woman,

and drank their fizzy lemonade.

As the people went on talking,

Tom and Tina

stuffed salted peanuts in their mouths.

After a while

a man reached for his glass.

"Cheers!"

The sweet fizzy drink

rinsed the salty taste

from their mouths.

It tasted horribly nice.

By a quarter to nine,

the lemonade bottle was empty,

and there were only salty crumbs

left in the peanut bag.

"Shall we go to bed?"
asked Tina, yawning.
Tom looked at his watch.
It's so silly to go
to bed early,
when you've been allowed
to stay up till nine.
"We'll wait another twenty minutes,
and then it'll be five past nine,"
said Tom.
Tina yawned.
Tom swivelled from side to side
in Father's favourite armchair.
Another twenty minutes.
How boring.
Tina tore a page from
the newspaper
and folded it
to make an aeroplane.

66

The plane whizzed across the room.
"Oh, that's stupid." said Tom
as it crash landed on his nose.
He got to his feet.
"It's so sticky and hot," he said
Boredom.
"Well, I'm going to bed,"
said Tina and threw
the paper plane
into the wastepaper basket.
"Me, too."

Tina lay in bed,
cuddling Floppy Ears,
and rubbed her nose
against his soft trunk.

Through the open window
a deep rumbling could be heard.
Tina opened her eyes.
The noise wasn't coming
from the garden.
It was in the clouds.

"Don't take any notice,
my little Floppy Ears!"
whispered Tina,
as she snuggled down in bed
and pressed the ears
of the stuffed elephant
close to its body.
White light flashed
through the room.
It made Tina jump
and she peeped out for an instant
from under the quilt.

68

She waited.

The thunder came rolling in

from a distance,

and Tina and Floppy Ears

disappeared under the quilt.

From under the covers

the rumbling

sounded a bit more friendly.

But no sooner had Tina

edged out again,

than another flash of lightning

appeared.

Tina held her breath and counted.

"One, two, three, four."

The thunder crashed

like a massive drum-beat.

Fergus whimpered.

He rattled the bars of his cot.

The storm was moving closer.

The thunder rumbled
like an iron marble
rolling over wooden boards.
From under the quilt
Tina could hear
her little brother crying.
She waited until the thunder
had stopped,
then she jumped out of bed
and dashed across to Fergus.
The baby stretched out his arms
to her, still crying.
She whisked him out of the cot,
and carried him over to her bed.
Another brilliant flash
of lightning.
Tina put Fergus down
on the mattress,
jumped into bed after him,

and pulled the quilt
over herself and her little brother.
Only just in time!
The crashing and banging outside
sounded like giants
doing a clog dance.
Tina reached for Fergus' hand.
His little fingers were soft and warm.
That felt better.
A storm isn't so bad
if you're not alone.
Very carefully Tina lifted the quilt.
Through screwed-up eyes
she squinted at the open window.

The billowing curtains flapped wildly
like flags in the wind.
"No, I'm not going to shut the window,"
thought Tina.
The next flash was blinding.
The thunder crashed. Tina felt it
right in the pit of her stomach.
Fergus cried
and Tina stroked his head.
"Don't cry, Fergus.
I'm frightened, too,"
she said, to comfort him.

Suddenly the quilt was whisked away.
"Help!" screamed Tina,
and clung to Fergus.
"It's only me."
Tom, in pyjamas,
was standing by the bed.

72

"I've come to protect you,"
he said.
With a bound,
Tom leapt into the bed,
and pulled the quilt
over himself, Tina and Fergus.

"Tom, we must shut the window."
"Oh, what for?" whispered Tom.
"To stop the rain getting in."
Thunder rumbled through the room.
Tom and Tina held their breath.
Fergus howled.
"We could shut the window
together,"
suggested Tom.
"All right, then," agreed Tina.
"On your marks, get set, go!"
The quilt flew in to the air.

Out of bed and over to the window.

The two big ones grabbed hold,

and, thank goodness,

the window closed.

"Stupid thunderstorm!" muttered Tom.

The lightning flashes

made them blink

and the thunder was deafening.

"I wish Father and Mother

were here,"

said Tina anxiously.

"We could crawl

under the bed

and take Fergus with us,"

Tom suggested.

Tina thought this over.

"Tom's right.

We must hide.

But under the bed isn't safe, either."

74

Lightning and, immediately, thunder.

No gap between the two.

"The storm is

right overhead now."

Tom's teeth were chattering.

Another crash, as if the walls

were falling down.

Secret hiding-place or no,

things were getting dangerous.

"Come quickly!" called Tina.

Shaking all over,

she ran to the wardrobe.

"Tom, bring Fergus!"

Tina climbed up on the chair

and took down the key.

The left-hand door creaked.

"What *are* you doing?" asked Tom.

He carried the whimpering Fergus

in his arms.

"We'll be safe here.
Quick, into the wardrobe!"
Tina pulled the door shut
behind them.
The winter clothes
had such a comforting smell.
The children crept through the clothes.
There wasn't much room.
Tina switched on the torch
and Tom was amazed.
"What a brilliant place, Tina!"
"This is my very secret
hiding-place."

Inside the wardrobe
the storm had faded
to a quiet rumble.

Tina shared out the caramels.

Fergus felt cosy
sitting between Tom and Tina.
Tina let him hold her doll.

"If you like, this can be
our secret hiding-
place now," said Tina.
"Great," laughed Tom,
and took a drink
of lemonade.

Outside, the thunder had stopped.
Instead, there was a ringing noise.
"Phone," whispered Tina.
All three crept out
of the wardrobe.
Tom switched on the light in the hall,
and answered the telephone.
It was Mother.

"No, the storm didn't
frighten us,"
said Tom proudly.
"Anyway, it's all over now.
Tina and I looked
after Fergus
very well."
Tom looked at Tina
and winked.
Tina winked back.